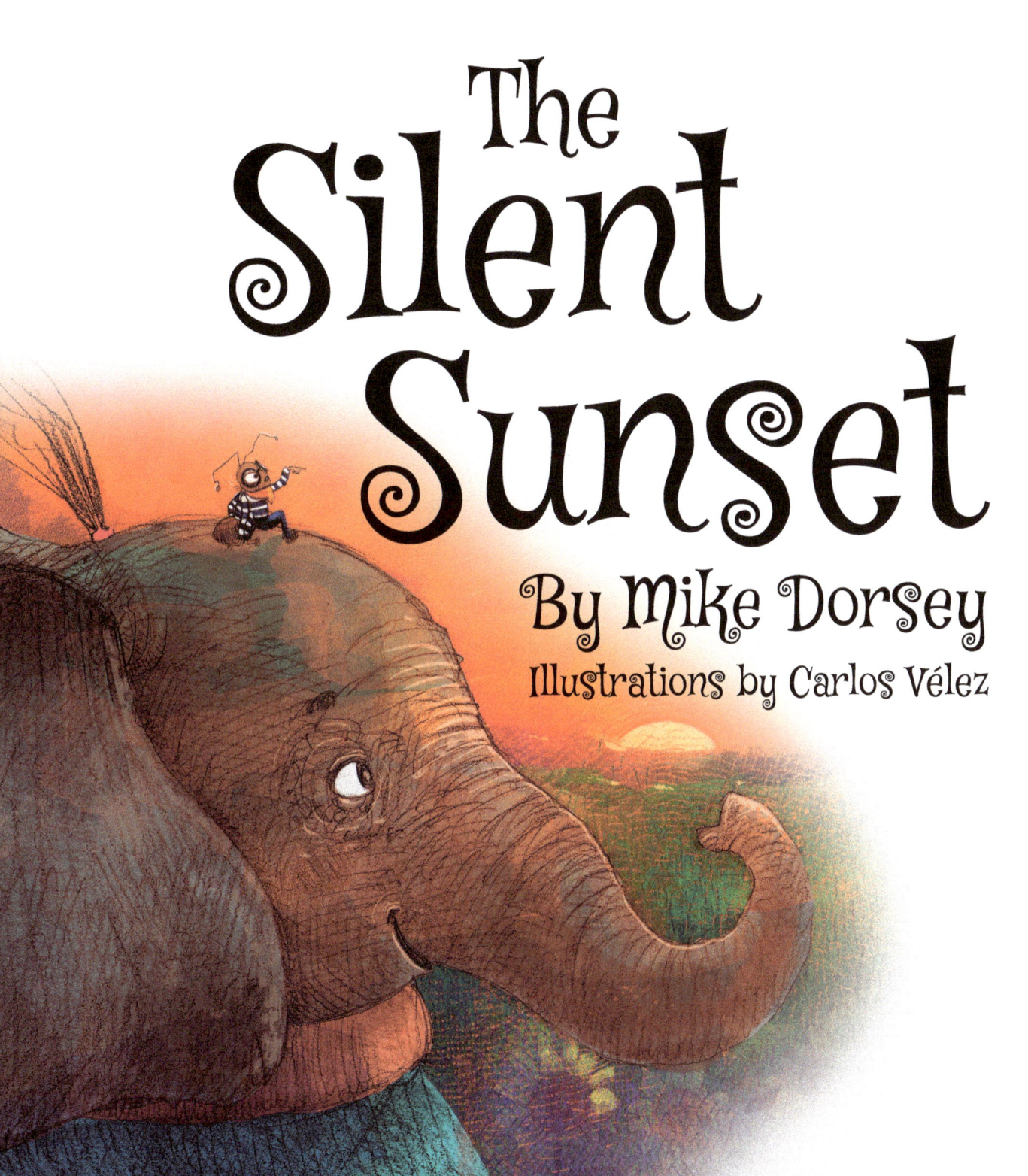

The Silent Sunset

By Mike Dorsey
Illustrations by Carlos Vélez

Copyright © 2022 by Michael Dorsey. All rights reserved.
This book may not be reproduced or stored in whole or in part
by any means without the written permission of the author
except for brief quotations for the purpose of review.

ISBN: 978-1-957723-36-5 (hard cover)
978-1-957723-37-2 (soft cover)

Edited by: Amy Ashby

Published by Warren Publishing
Charlotte, NC
www.warrenpublishing.net
Printed in the United States

*To all families with and without disabilities,
let's celebrate the sunsets of abilities.*

Emma the elephant loved looking at the sunset. It helped her forget her troubles as the only deaf animal—and the biggest student—at her school.

Sometimes kids were mean to her because they didn't understand what it was like to be different. Hearing about this, Emma's mother told her, "If you want to find joy in life, you have to look for it."
So, Emma set out to find something that made her happy.

One day Emma saw her mother looking at the sunset. She was amused as her mother stopped what she was doing and gasped. As Emma read her lips, her mother said out loud, "Look at that sunset! Every sunset is different than the next, yet they are all beautiful."

Emma decided that evening that she had found what made her happy: looking at sunsets. And from that moment on, she would do what her mother did; she would stop what she was doing, gasp, and look at the sunset with delight.

Anthony the ant loved looking at sunsets too. They helped him forget his troubles as the only one at his school who was hard of hearing. He also had cerebral palsy *and* was the smallest.

Some kids were mean to him because they didn't understand what it was like to be different. Hearing about this, his grandmother said, "The key to happiness is inside you. No one else can find it but you." So, Anthony set out to find something that made him happy.

One day Anthony saw a picture of his grandfather flying a plane through a sunset. The picture made him smile. And in that moment, Anthony knew he had found what made him happy: looking at sunsets—and airplanes.

Emma found a nice spot not far from her home to watch the sunset each night. On nights when her mother couldn't join her, she would often get lonely. So, just like she had many times before, she asked her older brother, Eli, to join her. "Eli, do you want to watch the sunset with me?"

Eli gave her the same answer: "Sorry, kiddo. I have to focus on making the best peanut butter cookies for the bakery contest that is coming in a few weeks." Emma was sad to go alone, but was happy to see the sunset.

Anthony found a nice spot not far from his home to watch the sunset each night. On nights when his grandmother couldn't join him, he would often get lonely. So, just like he had many times before, he asked his older sister, Antonia, to join him. "Antonia, do you want to watch the sunset with me?"

Antonia gave him the same answer: "Sorry, little brother. My friends and I are going to town where some boy dropped his ice cream scoop on the sidewalk in front of Ms. Antasia's nest. It's my favorite flavor—chocolate!" Anthony was sad to go alone, but was happy to see the sunset.

One evening on the way to see a sunset, Emma and Anthony bumped into each other. At first, they were frightened! Emma was so big and Anthony was so small. They were just so different.

Both of them signed, "Please don't mind me." When Emma and Anthony realized they both had signed, they jumped with joy. Neither of them had met another deaf animal before.

Emma then joked with Anthony, "I think we're meant to be friends. You can't spell 'elephant' without 'ant.'" Emma and Anthony laughed out loud.

Emma smiled and said, "Yes, I'm relieved too. I understand— it *is* hard. But you know what? Together, maybe you and I can try to bring others here."

Anthony shrugged his little shoulders and asked, "How are we going to do that? I can't even bring my own sister here. She always says she's busy."

Emma smiled and giggled. "Yes, I know! I can't bring my own brother to come here. He says he's too busy trying to make the best peanut butter cookies." She paused for a moment and scratched her chin. "Hey, wait a minute! I have an idea. Let's post flyers all over town saying there is an open mic night and a bake sale at this very spot to get people to come."

Anthony shouted with joy, "Yes!"

Emma then said, "Let's call the event: Sunset Festival."

"Yes! Great idea!" Anthony shouted.

Both Emma and Anthony worked hard together, creating flyers and hanging them up around town.

On the day of the Sunset Festival, Emma and Anthony sat at a table by the entrance to the park. Everyone was surprised to see that Emma and Anthony were the ones who had organized the festival.

When the sunset arrived, everyone couldn't help but to stop what they were doing and look at the beautiful shades of pink, purple, red, orange, yellow, and blue that radiated across the sky.

Emma noticed how Anthony struggled to see past everyone because he was so small. She smiled and said to him, "Why don't you climb on my head so you can see better?"

Anthony smiled and replied, "Thank you." Then, just as Anthony reached the top of Emma's head, he saw a plane fly through the sky and thought of his grandfather. He sighed. It was so nice to have more friends to share the sunset with.

And, for just a moment, everyone stared at something so quiet—and yet so beautiful—as they watched the silent sunset.

CPSIA information can be obtained
at www.ICGtesting.com
Printed in the USA
BVHW090625230622
640408BV00002B/7